Himalayan Folklore:
Ghosts and Demons
from
West Nepal

Oakley and Gairola
HIMALAYAN FOLKLORE:
GHOST AND DEMONS FROM WEST NEPAL

Ratna Folklore Series

No. IX

Himalayan Folklore:
Ghosts and Demons from West Nepal

E.S. Oakley and Tara Dutt Gairola

Adapted and edited by
Dipak Tuladhar and Suresh Shrestha

Ratna Pustak Bhandar
Kathmandu, Nepal

Himalayan Folklore:
Ghosts and Demons from West Nepal

Edition 2011

Published by Ratna Pustak Bhandar, Kathmandu, Nepal
Illustrated by Aakrin
© Publisher
Cover designed by Graphic Workshop
Printed in Nepal at Dongol Printers

ISBN: 978-99933-0-834-8

Acknowledgements

This collection is from *Himalayan Folklore: Kumaon and West Nepal*.* We have rewritten, edited and added illustrations thirteen tales from the last section of the book – Section II, Chapter V: Ghost and Demon Lore.

These lores were originally recorded from oral traditions handed down by generations of bards, or hurkia. These minstrels used to move about from one region to another, singing these folklores. They were the basic form of entertainment for the people of those days. We can guess how people have let their imaginations flow when the means of recreations were few, and traveling was difficult.

Some tales in this collection are similar, and some with slightly different versions are found in other countries. They are interesting as they all seem to have evolved from the common source in

---

* E.S. Oakley and Tara Dutt Gairola, *Himalayan Folklore: Kumaon and West Nepal* (1935), rep. in Bibliotheca Himalayica, Series II, Vol. 10, Ratna Pustak Bhandar (Kathmandu, 1977).

the past, as Rev. E.S. Oakley remarks in the introduction, which is reproduced here.

We hope the readers would appreciate our effort in presenting these stories in an easy readable format. We are thankful to Prof. Nirmal Man Tuladhar for this invaluable suggestions and to Kesar Lall whose many collections in his series inspired us.

D. Tuladhar

S. Shrestha

Contents

*Introduction**

The fact has often been remarked that almost all races, however remote from one another in place and time, and however little related in language, have practically much the same myths. The same may be said of the fairy tales and folklore of different countries. This has given rise to much speculation. Some have thought that the elements of folklore, representing such remarkable similarities, must be genealogically descended from ideas prevalent at a time when the human race was practically one, and undivided.

It is obviously impossible to trace such a connection historically, since we have nothing but the folk tales themselves to go upon; although it can be seen that the old Sanskrit stories, such as those contained in the *Panchtantra* and also many other stories, are the originals of much in the folklore of Asia and England. Much ingenuity was wasted in

---

* E.S. Oakley and Tara Dutt Gairola, *op. cit.*, pp. 173–179.

the last half century on attempts to show the descent for fables philologically; and an Indian origin was ascribed in the elaborate speculations of Max Muller, Sir G. Coxe and others, to Greek and Roman mythology. Sanskrit etymologies were expected to explain everything. More recent inquirers have realized that etymology does not really explain the origin of a myth or fable. A more real solution to the puzzle is found in the reflection that all races began at the same mental level, and human nature from the beginning being a constant quantity, the same ideas, in almost the same forms, were evolved in various countries, representing the attempt of early man to formulate some theory of the natural appearances around him. Many of these are incredibly rude and gross even in the beautiful mythology of Greece. It is not because some deep spiritual meaning is concealed beneath the rude form, but because they faithfully reflect the ideas of early men, handed down in a modified form to a more refined age in which they appear as strange survivals, like Pan and the Fauns and Satyrs, presenting themselves in the company of well-bred ladies and gentlemen.

In the folk tales of every land, we have survivals of the primitive conception of the world and the forces of nature. In this connection it is not easy to distinguish between mythology and folklore; for both represent an early stage of consciousness when man's fancy worked with freedom and was employed to give an explanation of all things. We are apt to think too seriously of the so-called religious ideas of non-Christian peoples. They are largely relics of man's early unrestrained fancy, consecrated, to some extent, in later times, by custom and priestly adoption; but, originally, on the same level as our nursery tales. To the early intelligence of our remote ancestors everything was alive. Life was a constant surprise, and miracles happened every hour. Nothing was inconceivable, because everything was possible. Hence the wonderful richness of fancy which characterizes these early pictures. Hence also the peculiar ascription of life to all kinds of objects.

A savage state even now exists in some countries to which the name of Animism and Fetishism have been applied. The vivid sense of life as existing everywhere, combined with a vague and confused idea as to what constitutes life and soul, gave rise to the notions familiar to us in our commonest fables and folk tales. We may take for example the idea of a magician's soul or life as something which he can hide away in order to keep it safe from enemies, but whose hiding-place the hero of the story discovers, with fatal consequences to the wizard. This is said to be a real belief among some savage tribes existing today. In Mr. W. B. Yeats' charming review of Irish folk tales there is a story about the souls of drowned sailors being kept in lobster pots at the bottom of the sea; and when these were turned up the souls escaped. In *Grim's Fairy Tales* we read of the house of Death where the souls of men burn as candles, and when one goes out a life ceases. In the same book we read of a child's soul being present in a rose which blossomed afresh when the child died; and of another child whose life was identified with that of a toad the killing of which caused it to die also.

A manuscript collection of Himalayan folk tales has come into the writer's possession, made a good many years ago, by an Indian official in Garhwal. It is interesting to come across a story in which the familiar feature above mentioned finds a place. The story is given below exactly as told by the peasants of Garhwal in the long winter evenings.

In an island beyond the seven seas there lived a demon who had a beautiful daughter. A certain prince, hearing of her beauty, fell in love with her fame and set off to gain her hand in marriage. It took him six months to travel to the island, but at last he arrived there and found a large and beautiful city adorned with gold, silver and precious stones, but with no human beings in its streets. The inhabitants of the city had all been devoured by the fiend.

At length, after wandering about the place for some hours, he espied the princess sitting at a window of the royal place. He approached and entered into conversation with her. She earnestly advised him to go away at once, saying: 'Wretched mortal, what ill fate has brought thee here only to be devoured by my father who is even now gone to hunt for human prey? You will surely fall into his clutches unless you escape quickly, for no man who visits this barren island is ever spared by him. He can traverse a hundred miles in a few minutes. You had better be off with all speed.'

The prince replied, 'Beautiful Lady, I have come hither for your sake only. After passing through all manner of dangers and hardships I cannot forsake you now, even should I be eaten by your father. I shall willingly die in the attempt to gain you.'

The princess, touched by his devotion, then showed him some gourds which the demon had filled with different articles intended for his own defense. The first contained mist, and the second thorns, the third water, the fourth mountains. By means of these the demon hoped to be able to escape from every adversary. She also showed the prince an iron cage in which a parrot was kept, and in the parrot was the demon's life. She then instructed him how he should proceed when attacked by the demon.

As soon as the prince had taken the gourds in his hands, the fiend felt sick and giddy, his life being threatened; and perceiving that an attempt was being made to destroy him, he ran homewards. The prince thereupon dashed down the mist gourd, which spread darkness in his path. Then he broke the thorn gourd, the water gourd, the mountain gourd, one after another, and these threw obstacles in his way and hindered his approach to the house. Yet, in spite of all these hindrances, he was making his way rapidly homewards. When he had come quite near, the prince severed the legs of the parrot with his sword, and immediately the demon fell down. He, however, managed to drag along his body over the ground towards his enemy. But just as he was about to close with the prince, the latter killed the parrot outright, whose death at once caused that of the demon. The prince married the daughter, and returned triumphantly to his own country, taking with him his beautiful bride.

Another story embodies the same idea, and mentions also a profusion of magical properties which would be exceedingly useful to any official on tour, such as a fairy flute, flying bed, a self-tying rope, and an automatic club, a self-cooking pot and an auto-distributing spoon. The wizard's life was concealed in an insect inhabiting the body of a parrot kept in an iron cage, which again was secured in an innermost chamber, there being six outer rooms carefully padlocked leading to it, and the keys of these rooms were kept by the magician himself. As soon as the hero (who in this case also was the lover of the wizard's daughter) opened the first room, the wizard felt feverish, when the second room was unlocked, he had high fever. The magic flute when played called down a number of heavenly nymphs (Apsaras, it is to be presumed), who danced bewitchingly and produced a shower of celestial flowers (Parijat flowers) which have wonderful properties.

E.S. Oakley

The Kayasth and
the Demon

A Kayasth travelling in search of a livelihood arrived in a city late in the evening. Finding no place to stay, he stayed in a deserted house outside the city, which was said to be haunted and abandoned by its owners. The Kayasth, ignorant of it, occupied it.

As soon as he finished preparing some food and a strong drink, a hungry demon with dreadful features appeared. The poor Kayasth, already frightened with his ghastly looks,

served all the food to him including the drink. The demon devoured it leaving nothing for the scared Kayasth. The food and specially the drink seemed to pacify the demon.

The demon said to him, 'Why have you come here?'

He replied, 'Sir, I have come here for a job.'

The demon said, 'You stay here and prepare delicious food for me every evening. Every morning, you will find two rupees under the lamp to purchase groceries and salary for your service.'

The desperate Kayasth accepted the offer and started cooking meals for the demon. He sent the savings home. The demon would appear for supper in the evening and disappear in the morning. Earning enough for his livelihood by his service to the monster, the Kayasth enjoyed serving him for a long time.

One evening, he asked the demon for permission to go home. The demon granted and gave him a large reward and three strands of his moustache. He told him he would come to his help at any time whenever he would burn a strand of his moustache. Next morning the man left for his home.

During his visit, the king of his country was overthrown and the kingdom taken over by the enemy. The king fled to the forest. The Kayasth went and offered his help. The king laughed at his offer, considering the difficult task ahead. The Kayasth took out a strand of the demon's moustache. As soon as he put it in the fire he appeared.

The Kayasth told the demon about the misfortunes of his king. The demon produced thousands of demons like him and drove out the enemy of the king. The grateful king divided his kingdom into two parts and gave the half to the Kayasth as a reward for his services.

The Kayasth thus became a king with the help of the demon.

The Prince and the Enchanted Sword

A prince proposed to a beautiful princess. But the princess replied:

'Oh Prince, I cannot accept your proposal unless you procure me a beautiful tank on the bank of which is a terrace paved with copper sheets, silver stairs leading to it, with a gold throne placed in its centre in the shade of a tree with emerald leaves, topaz buds, diamond flowers, pearl fruits, which I saw in my dream.'

The prince immediately set out in search of such a scene. After wandering through various forests and remote places he saw a saint in the jungle. Fearful of approaching, the prince stayed at a distance in a secluded corner.

But the saint had noticed him and enquired: 'What is the purpose of your coming to the jungle?'

The prince replied: 'Sir, I have a great longing for marrying a beautiful princess, but she will not accept my proposal until I secure the object of her dream which is – a beautiful tank of crystal water, on the bank of which has a terrace paved with copper plates, silver stairs leading to it, a gold throne placed on the centre of the terrace, together with a shining tree of emerald leaves, topaz buds, diamond flowers, and pearl fruits, which the princess saw in her dream. She wishes to receive this from the person who wishes to marry her. So I have been roaming here and there in the jungles for many months in search of such a place.'

The saint said, 'Dear Prince, I can give you a clue to such a tank. But it is very difficult for a human to obtain it unless he fasts for several days and nights before going to the place where it exists.'

The prince said, 'Sage, I am ready to do whatever you say at any cost of bodily and mental pain.'

The saint said, 'Go to the east with this enchanted sword. There, you fast. On the eighth day, seven fairies will come to bath in the tank one after another. As soon as the first fairy has bathed, behead her with this sword; she will turn into a copper terrace; then do the same to the second fairy, who will turn into silver stairs leading to the copper bank. Follow with the third fairy, who will turn into the emerald tree, then fourth, who will become a throne of gold, the fifth fairy will turn into topaz buds, the sixth into diamond flowers, the seventh into pearl fruits. Be firm and bold in the pursuit of your goal. Goodbye and best of luck!'

The prince set out at once. He arrived at the lake and fasted for seven days. On the eighth day, he beheaded the fairies one by one as they came to bathe in the lake. Thus, the lake turned into the beautiful tank as the princess had dreamed of.

He brought the princess to the place. The princess, seeing her dream tank, became very happy and accepted the prince's proposal.

3

The Prince and the Demon's Daughter

There lived a demon in an island beyond the seven seas. He had a beautiful daughter. A prince was fascinated by her beauty and set out to marry her. The journey to the island took six months.

On his arrival in the island, he saw a big and beautiful city full of gold, silver and precious stones but devoid of human beings. The demon had devoured all the city dwellers. He saw the girl of his love, sitting alone at a

window of a big palace. She advised him to go away at once, and said:

'Human, what evil fortune brought you here, only to be devoured by my father, who has just gone out to hunt for human beings and animals? He will not spare you. He can trail human being's scent and walk hundreds of miles in few strides. Run away as swiftly as you can.'

The prince replied, 'Oh! My love, I have come here for your sake, facing many hardships. I cannot leave you now whether you kill me or your father eats me up.'

She was moved by his determination, and she showed him for gourds kept by the demon that protected him. The first gourd contained mist, the second thorns, the third water and the fourth mountains. There was also an iron cage with a parrot. The parrot contained the soul of the demon. She also explained in detail how to kill her father.

No sooner had the prince taken the four gourds, then the devil felt giddy. Realizing that an attempt was being made against his life, he ran home. The prince broke the mist gourd which created darkness on the devil's way. Then he broke the gourds with the thorn, the water and the mountain spells one after the other. All these brought up obstacles and blocked his way home.

In spite of all these hindrances, he kept running home. When he reached near home, the prince severed the parrot's two legs and the demon became lame. Yet, he dragged his body along to face the enemy. As the demon was close to the prince, he killed the parrot and the demon fell dead.

The prince married the demon's daughter and returned home with his beautiful bride in glory.

4

The Prince and the Celestial Flowers

A king, who had lost his queen, was banished from his kingdom by another ruler. He retreated to the forest with his two sons and resorted to selling firewood in the city for livelihood.

The younger prince, finding the work tedious and also lowly, went on his own way. He hid his true identity, pretending to be a dumb man and became a servant of the banker and worked competently.

The banker's son was in love with the king's daughter and planned to elope with her. He stole money, jeweleries and precious stones and send them a head loaded on ponies. When he was about to leave, the servant caught him and locked him up with the permission of the banker. He then sought to bring back the riches his son had secretly stashed.

Assuming that the banker's son had set out, the princess also left the palace. The princess and the servant arrived in a town in the evening. The princess was afraid of the servant, but having no one else to help her, she accepted the lodging and provision arranged by him. They slept together but placed a dagger between them as a pledge of chastity.

Next day, he returned the loot to the banker. He then went to the king and handed back his daughter. The king was pleased with him for preventing an embarrassing royal scandal and offered him employment in the palace. So he became a personal servant of the king with high salary. These special privileges made him an object of envy among the other staff members of the royal household. So they started spreading false rumours. Influenced by them the king punished the dumb servant by ordering him to bring the flowers of *parijat* for him. The task was impossible for human beings.

After arranging the necessary preparation, he set out for the impossible task. While on journey, he came to a deserted town with only one girl living in it. He befriended her and played *chauparh*, a kind of board game, with her. In the evening, she told him to go away otherwise her father, a demon, would devour him. The prince told her he could not part with her even for any kind of danger to his life. She changed him into a fly.

When the demon came home, he cried out 'Human scent!'

She told him he had already eaten all the people except her. The next day after the demon had gone hunting, she changed the fly back into the prince. In this way, they enjoyed each other's company for months. So engrossed and infatuated was he that he even forgot his mission to procure the *parijat* flowers.

One day he told her she had to choose between him and her father. She replied she would get rid of her father instead.

She said to her father, 'I am very anxious for you, I hear your brother, in disguise, has come here to kill you. How can you defend yourself against him?'

The demon replied, 'My dear, don't worry about my life. I cannot be killed by anyone in the world. My soul is secured in the body of the

beetle, which is secured in the parrot's body, which is kept in an iron cage. This cage is further secured in the innermost room of six outer rooms with padlocks. The keys of all those locks are with me.'

The girl eagerly asked him further:

'What if you lose the keys? So will you leave the keys in my care during your absence for my peace of mind?'

He consented and gave her the keys. She again said, 'Father, I am always expecting your coming home. Will you kindly tie a bell around your neck so that I hear the ringing when you get home for my relief? I always worry about you.'

The demon agreed with her request. The next day, after the demon had left for hunting, they opened the first room, the demon felt feverish; on unlocking the second room made him weak. Realizing he had been deceived by his own daughter, he ran home. Hearing the tinkling of the bell the girl and the prince hurriedly opened the rest of the doors. They captured the parrot from the cage, killed it, ripped its body open and also killed the beetle inside. That was the end of the demon.

The girl married the prince and wished to go with him. He remembered his mission and said:

'My love, I have to fulfill a promise to the king (whose servant I am) to bring the celestial flowers; so you must remain here, until I bring the flowers for my king. Will you enlighten me as how to procure this heavenly flowers?'

She said, 'Very well. Go to the remotest jungles which are inhabited by ascetics, and they will be able to give instructions as to where and how the flowers can be obtained.'

He went deep into the woods and met a fakir, who was known for possession of a magical flying bed. He asked about the flowers. The ascetic told him that the flowers were available in the heaven or in the hell and advised him to continue the journey onward.

He met another ascetic, who had a magical self-cooking pot and a self-serving spoon. He also told the prince to go further ahead. Then he met a dervish, who protected himself with his special self-striking club and the self-binding rope, and this ascetic told him that on a certain night, all the gods and fairies would descend on the earth and dance to the tune of a flute played by another celestial being, and whenever he played the flute, the *parijat* flowers would rain down on them. They would disappear next morning. He was advised to go there and take the opportunity to collect as many flowers as he wanted.

He reached the place that night and saw the gods and fairies dancing to the flute's tunes. They vanished as the celestial person playing the music disappeared at day break, but forgot to take the flute. The prince took the flute instead of the flowers. He went back to the dervish who had informed him about this heavenly event earlier, and showed it. He demonstrated what it could do. He was ecstatic and expressed a desire to receive the magical flute in exchange for the self-striking club and the self-binding rope.

As soon as he possesed these magical items, the cunning prince commanded them to beat and bind the fakir and took back the flute. He met the second dervish and showed the flute and explained its magical power. The ascetic was enchanted and asked for it in exchange for his invaluable self-cooking pot and self-serving spoon. The prince bartered his flute for magical pot and spoon and resumed his way. He then ordered the club and rope to overpower the dervish. This order was immediately carried out; he took the flute back.

Then he went back to the first fakir, showed him the flute and related how he had obtained it. He wanted it too and offered his flying bed in exchange. He readily agreed with the deal and gave him the flute. As soon as he left the place, mounting the self-flying bed, he ordered his

club and rope to get his flute back from the fakir. The command was instantly carried out.

He went to his wife. With all his invaluable magical possessions, they flew to the king's palace on the flying bed. He arranged a show for the king that night. He played the flute and the fairies appeared and danced bewitchingly pouring celestial flowers down on them. The king and his retinue were fascinated with the extraordinary and amazing scene and the whole assembly heartily thanked and congratulated him on his incredible achievement. The king asked him what he would like for his reward.

He then revealed his true identity and asked for king's daughter in marriage for his elder brother.

Next day, he rode the flying bed with his wife, the princess and his riches, and arrived in his own country. He conquered back his lost kingdom with the help of the club and the rope. He put his elder brother on the throne and served as a minister. He married the princess and his elder brother. He then formally married the demon's daughter, who was trained in a hundred and eight arts.

The Ghost and
the Sick Man

Years ago, a postman arrived in a house at night where he found a sick man lying on a bed, with no one else caring for him. The sick man welcomed him and said he could spend the night with him there. The food was available but he would have to prepare it himself. The host was too ill to get up.

He lighted the fire and began to cook, doing everything by himself. He forgot to take salt to the kitchen. (It is forbidden for a Hindu to come out of the kitchen when the food is being

cooked in the Kumaon hills.) He told the sick man that he had not taken salt with him and asked him if he could pass it on to him.

The sick man stretched out his hand all the way from his bed to reach for the salt and give it to him.

This extraordinary sight terrified him, and at once he ran away leaving behind all his belongings. Strangely, the sick man chased him for some distance.

The postman reached another village at midnight fully exhausted and spent the rest of the night there. Next day, he with some villagers went back to the house of the sick man to take his belongings.

They found the sick man lying on the bed dead and they also noticed that flowers of mustard were sticking out from his toes. The dead man had chased him through the mustard fields the other night.

On further inquiry with the neighbours, he came to know that all the residents of the house had died of epidemic disease. All of them were cremated by the surviving members of the family. The one, who died last, was not taken away for cremation, and this deprived him of his last rites. Thus, his spirit was still lingering around and everyone was afraid to approach the house.

The postman was very lucky to have escaped from the claws of the dead.

The Magical Contest

A childless Brahmin went to a jogi (ascetic), and implored him to bless him with children. The latter, after giving him some medicinal herbs, demanded the first-born must become his disciple. The Brahmin agreed to the condition.

In course of time, the Brahmin was blessed with two sons. The jogi appeared after some years to remind the Brahmin of his promise. The Brahmin kept his word and requested the ascetic to train his younger son too. The jogi reluctantly agreed and took both the sons.

The jogi began teaching his art to both alike, but excluded the younger from the specialized teachings. This was conducted in a room which was shut to the younger one, supposing the elder son to be his real disciple.

The younger disciple was hurt and angry with his teacher's partiality but he was smart and inquisitive. He secretly learned by standing close to the door and attentively listening to what was being taught to his brother.

Once the ascetic gave a wooden bowl to each of the brothers to be oiled. The elder begged for oil and butter from door to door and got the bowl oiled a little bit. The younger one had a better plan. He purchased bowlful of oil on credit and returned it the next day claiming it to be of bad quality and got the bowl fully greased in the process without any expense.

The jogi, noticing the younger disciple too clever for his liking, found an excuse to send him back home when he was caught eavesdropping during one of the secret classes to his elder disciple.

This only heightened his hatred towards the jogi and hatched a plan to kill him. He told his father that he would turn into a majestic mare, which he should give it as gift to the jogi. The

boy transformed into a mare and the father took it to the jogi.

The jogi at once recognized the mare to be the shrewd boy. He turned it over to his disciple (the elder brother) with the instruction that it should get enough fodder and water but always locked up, and not to be taken out.

The disciple acted according to the instruction for a considerable time. One day, forgetting his guru's strict directive, took the mare to a river for a wash. No sooner had the mare touched the water of the river it turned into a fish and then disappeared.

On hearing this, the infuriated jogi took the form of a fisherman to catch the fish. The fish then turned into a bee, the fisherman became a hornet to kill it. The bee then transformed into one of the pearls in the necklace worn by the daughter of the king of the country. On feeling some sensation, the princess threw the necklace on the pavement of the palace.

The jogi changed himself into a cock and began to eat the scattered pearls. Just before the pearl as about to be devoured, he transformed himself into a cat, and killed the cock.

Thus the boy got his revenge for the prejudiced behaviour of his master.

The Ghost and
the Four Women

There was a well-to-do man in a village. One night, the hunting party of a king reached the village very tired. The wealthy man hosted them well.

Next morning, they went to the king and told him about the man's vast amount of wealth he possessed. Instead of appreciating his hospitality the iniquitous ruler ordered his servants to seize the man's wealth. They carried out his order.

The man, his wife, four sons and their wives left the house with hardly anything in their possession. The wife of the youngest son had concealed sixteen gold coins on her body. When they felt hungry, the woman gave the father-in-law one gold coin to purchase food. The man went to buy food but did not return. She gave another coin to her mother-in-law and she also did not return. Then the four sons were also given a gold coin each. But all of them did not return too. It was assumed they all died somehow.

The four women were left to fend for themselves, and decided to work. First, they purchased male clothes to conceal their identity and wore it with turbans to hide their braided hair. They accepted the employment in the court of the wicked king, and appeared tidy and energetic young men, worthy of service in every way. They served him for a considerable time without raising suspicion.

One night, the only son of the king died and they were ordered to carry out the prince's last rites. They took the body to the crematorium, despite the fear of the ghost who was said to appear at night and frighten those who would encounter it.

No sooner had they arrived than the ghost with dreadful features appeared. One of the women clung to the ghost, undauntedly holding the matted hair firmly. After a daring fight, joined in by her three sisters-in-law, the vanquished spirit yielded. They would not set the ghost free unless they were given whatever they demanded. Being completely overpowered, the ghost pledged to do whatever they wanted. First, they ordered the ghost to bring back to life the dead prince. The spirit brought the prince to life. Next, they demanded the ghost to revive their husbands and their parents. The ghost carried out this too.

When the four disguised women did not return to the palace that night, the king sent his servants to look for them. They found the prince alive and learned about the miracle that had happened. They went back and told the king immediately.

The king did not believe his courtiers and went himself to see. He was overjoyed to find his son alive. In return, he gladly gave half his kingdom to the family of the four brave and clever women to repent of the wrongdoings he had committed against them.

The Dead Man
Who Moved and Talked

A man and his wife lived in a house in the midst of a dense forest with their livestock. One night, the man fell ill and died. The next morning, the man's relative came by for a visit. As soon as he arrived, the dead man began to move and talk.

The wife, who had found him dead the other night, was happy to see him alive on the arrival of his kinsman.

In gratitude, she said with folded hands: 'Dear kinsman, I have no proper words to say

about the recovery of my husband, who was dead last night, but no sooner have you arrived than he is alive. You are the giver of new life.'

The relative was also delighted. The woman asked him what food he preferred. Her husband intervened, and said:

'I and my kinsman will not take our meal now, but at night together. You must go at once to a neighbouring village to invite the people here tomorrow morning as I wish to see them on account of the joy I feel at my new life.'

The wife went as directed. They ate nothing during the day. In the evening, the man told his kinsman to prepare food. While the food was being cooked, salt was required and asked the man to pass it on. The man stretched his hand to a place (where salt was kept) five meters from his bed and reached for the salt.

This supernatural deed of the man frightened the kinsman and ran away, knowing the man was actually dead and now had become a ghost. He fled to the shed and embraced a cow there. It is believed that the cows being holy the ghosts and demons fear to approach them.

The next morning when the wife came home with the people of the neighbouring village, they found her husband dead and the kinsman clinging onto a cow in the shed. The man had died the first time after all but his spirit wanted to stay on as a ghost to haunt.

Together, they cremated the dead man.

The Ghost and
the Firewood

A traveler arrived at a *ghat*, (a crematorium) in the evening. He collected some firewood on the bank of a river.

He lighted the firewood and cooked his food. After eating, he slept near the fire for warmth.

At midnight, a number of ghosts appeared, crying, 'Give us our fuel! Give us our fuel!'

He was frightened and ran away to a neighbouring village, leaving everything behind.

No one takes remaining of the crematorium wood as it is considered the property of the ghosts.

The Ghost in the Mill

A man came to a water-mill for grinding his grain. He had to lodge for the night in a nearby shed as it became late because the water-mill kept stopping repeatedly as if by some unnatural force while his grain was being ground.

This shed was on the bank of a river which was used as a crematorium. At midnight, a strange man entered the shed, and asked the man:

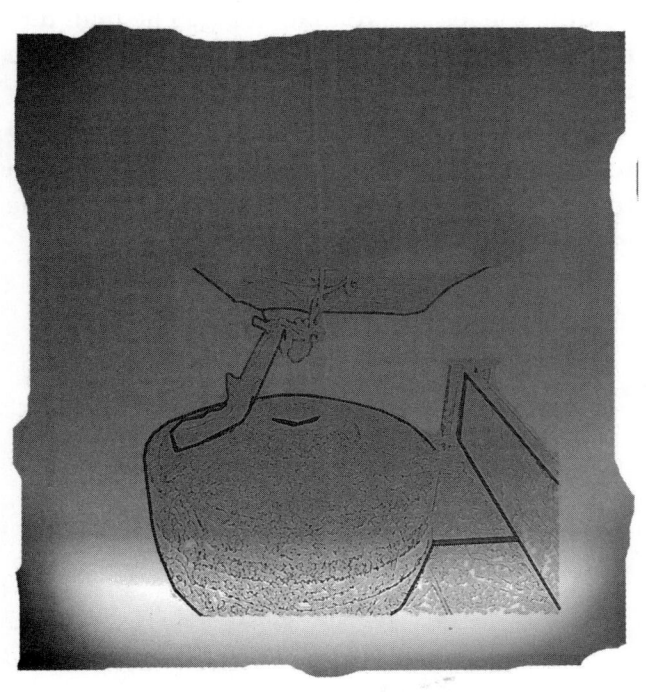

'Do you like to eat meat?'

The man replied yes but he suspected the stranger to be a ghost. As soon as the ghost turned his back, the man started shivering with fear and ran away to his village, leaving his grain behind in the mill. The ghost chased him, holding the leg of a human being. The man had made a good head start. The ghost pursued him up to the village, but could not enter his house.

He went with other villagers next morning to the water-mill to bring his grain; he was so terrified by last night's encounter with the ghost he dared not go there alone again.